I0720038

Cupid: An Alien Scifi Romance

DEMELZA CARLTON

ONE

Orel took a deep breath, then forced it out slowly. He couldn't delay any longer – it was now or never. He'd seen Anna head into the staff break room only a minute ago, and if he waited any longer, someone else would venture in there for a coffee, and he'd miss his chance.

Now, man, now!

He stumbled on the first step, then righted himself and kept going. If he missed this chance, he'd be letting Cupid's curse win.

Orel rounded the corner, drawing in another breath, before he said, "Oh, hi, Anna. I was wondering…"

She turned around, and he stopped dead at the sight of tears streaming down her face. Silent tears, because if he'd heard her crying, he wouldn't have barged in here and…

"What's wrong?" he asked instead.

She smiled through her tears. The first real smile he'd ever seen on her face in the year he'd worked with her. Possibly her first smile since her husband's death. "Oh, nothing," she said, swiping at her cheeks. "I've just had the most wonderful news, and I can barely believe it. After all this time…it turns out my husband was still alive, in an escape pod. A salvage crew found him and the hospital wants me there when he wakes up. Valentine's alive, Orel, and I get him back on Valentine's Day. I'm so happy I could…cry." A fresh flood of tears washed down her cheeks, but there was no mistaking that joyful smile.

How could he be anything but happy for

her?

"That's amazing news," he blurted out. "What did old Earth mystics call it? A miracle, that's what this is. It's not often the universe brings someone back from the dead."

She laughed softly and wiped her eyes. "We bring the dead back to life every day here, or at least I do. Have you never been into my lab, or the Lost World Biome? I can give you a tour or maybe you could even work a day with me next week, if you like. I'm sure someone else could cover your duties for a day."

Orel found himself nodding politely, not wanting to ruin her day with his whining. A concussed monkey could cover his duties most days here in Eden. If the robot rebellion in the Titan system could have waited a few more weeks, he'd have finished his MBA and he wouldn't have to work as a glorified gopher. If they'd waited another year, he'd have been able to pocket a tidy profit from the first year's sales of Professor Poulet's latest chimera.

But they hadn't, and then Poulet had

perished on the *Titanic,* so now he was the Eden Labs errand boy, at the beck and call of everyone who had a PhD, especially…

"Oh, hello, Lilith."

"Hi, Anna. Have you seen Orel anywhere?"

Lilith entered the break room.

Anna gave a little wave and left.

"There you are! Rocail's on the warpath, because your bloody birds are still in his biome, when he wanted it for his project yesterday!" Lilith said.

If Eden Labs had a prima donna, it was Rocail, though he was definitely no lady. Orel wasn't sure what Lilith saw in him, but he knew better than anyone that love could blossom in the strangest places, so he kept his opinions to himself. Perhaps Rocail had redeeming features he showed to no one else but Lilith.

"I told Dr Rocail I'd have the birds out for farm testing by the end of today. If he'd told me before 4am this morning that he wanted that biome, I might have been able to meet his timeline, but as it is…" Orel shrugged. "I can't work miracles, or time travel. I had intended to have my lunch break first before I did the afternoon deliveries, but if it's so urgent, perhaps I could do the deliveries first…"

Lilith's tensed shoulders dropped as her breath hissed out. "Thank you. I…he's…you know how he is. Especially about his top secret projects."

Orel did. He also knew more about those top secret projects than most of the other staff, because he'd had to procure all manner of strange things for Rocail's projects. Always with impossible deadlines he could never meet, so it was no wonder everyone in Eden believed he was an incompetent idiot. Never mind that he met Rocail's demands nine times out of ten, which was more than anyone else could do. No, he was stuck here in Eden, because he'd never get a good reference from anyone here that would let him get another job anywhere.

"I'll get right on it, Dr Lilith," Orel said. "If you could tell Rocail his biome will be ready and sanitised by the end of the day?"

Lilith nodded, worry creasing her forehead again. "I will, but he won't like it."

She hurried out before Orel could form a reply. Probably a good thing, or he might have been tempted to tell her to dump Rocail and find someone who made her smile instead of stress. Lilith was an intelligent woman – she'd work it out for herself eventually. He hoped.

As Orel headed for the birds' biome, he pulled out his tablet to schedule a thorough clean for it. He figured he could get the birds caged up and out of there in less than an hour, so setting the wash cycle to start in sixty minutes seemed reasonable.

Twenty-three minutes later, Orel smugly guided the hovercart of crated birds out of Eden and on their way to their new homes.

Professor Poulet, may the stars rest his soul, would have been proud. A pity he'd never lived long enough to see these chimeras reach their final stage of testing. Once they'd passed this, they'd be ready for full commercialisation

on every planet, station and ship in the Altan
system.

TWO

"I agreed to have chickens in my garden. Those don't look like chickens."

"What's that on its back?"

"Are they supposed to be green?"

"What did you say they're called again?"

Every time Orel released the chimeras from their box, the questions started flying. Every single person who'd agreed to accept a flock knew that they were experimental, engineered birds from Eden, found nowhere on Earth, but the moment they saw them…

Orel sighed.

"We call them chicken salads," he'd explained to Ghost, as he backed out of the specially constructed pen in the man's garden in the Arbor Dome. It looked like it was made from the surrounding trees, but timber was too precious to waste on livestock. Synthwood, most likely, which didn't smell as fragrant as trunks that had once been full of sap. Or those that still were, crowding around him as if to listen to his explanation. "They're genetically engineered chickens that are both a food source and an enhancement to normal waste disposal facilities aboard a space ship or station. In fact, they're currently thriving on many Titan ships, as we speak."

"Are they safe for my son?" Ghost demanded.

Orel hesitated. The chimeras behaved like ordinary chickens, which meant they pecked and scratched like any of their Earth counterparts. "The food they produce is as safe as anything else grown here in the Colony, but they are animals, which will defend themselves if they are manhandled. A peck or a scratch, or maybe a wing buffet. How old is your son?"

"Only six weeks, but everyone keeps telling me kids grow so fast, he'll be walking before I know it, and into everything." He looked both excited and alarmed at the prospect.

If Ghost thought Human babies grew fast, he should see the herd of cows at Byron's ranch. Scant months ago, they'd been newborn calves wobbling around on unfamiliar legs, but they were now almost full grown and grazing on the grasses that grew in the arid soils in the farms beneath the Arena Dome.

"Yes, they're supposed to be green," Orel had told Byron and his partner, Rana, trying not to cough in the dust the cows had kicked up when they'd seen him and stampeded off. Evidently they remembered him from Eden, expecting him to give chase, but he didn't have time to play today. "They're a lot like Earth chickens, just…engineered to undergo photosynthesis, hence the leaves on its back. Those are edible, by the way, like a kind of leaf lettuce. I'm not sure how well they'll do in the dry heat here – the leaves, that is, not the birds. As long as the birds get enough water and food, they'll be fine. In space, they use those leaves to make energy when food is scarce."

Food wasn't likely to be scarce for the chimeras here in the Colony, whether in Ghost's forest, Byron's desert or the tropical plantation Phoebe maintained where she planned to raise her chicken salads.

Entering the farming level beneath the Aqua Dome was always a rude shock. Unlike the dry, dusty heat that blasted him in the face when he stepped onto Byron's ranch, the plantation humidity landed on his shoulders, pressing him down like one of the large parrots in the Amazon Biome, or the ghost of heavier gravity in the greenhouses back on Tito. Greenhouses that were gone now.

Across the river lay Paddy's Farm, as Triton

called his rice terraces, though Phoebe insisted on calling the whole place the Grove.

Her chicken salads would have free range throughout her plantation, so Orel released the birds among the trees, under Phoebe's watchful eyes. She simply nodded serenely at his spiel about the birds, their care and anything else she needed to know.

"And if there's any issues, call me and I'll be right over," Orel finished.

"What are those things? If they come across the river and start ripping up my crop, I'll turn them into fertiliser!" Triton stood on the riverbank, eyes flaming as he fixed his gaze on the green chimeras.

"Chickens won't go anywhere near your flooded fields," Phoebe said scornfully. "They like their soil dry, so it's easier to scratch around in. And they eat the bugs that proliferate in that foetid swamp you call a farm!" Her green eyes flashed, though nowhere near as luminously as Triton's.

Triton scraped his shoe on the grassy bank,

as if trying to rid it of something he'd stepped in. For a moment, he looked like a horse pawing the ground. "At least my farm's producing something. How many more years before your trees do more than just suck up water and shed leaves?"

Most of the Colony's trees, including Phoebe's plantation, were established at the end of the war, soon after the domes were sealed. After four years of accelerated growth, Orel was surprised they weren't fruiting already. He squinted at the nearest tree. Actually...

"This year. They're hard to see now, but once they ripen, those mangoes will stand out so even your dull eyes won't be able to miss them," Phoebe said smugly.

"Hmph!" Triton stalked away.

Orel thought he glimpsed hurt in the other man's eyes before he turned away. He'd better head off, too, before he started imagining something between these two that ran deeper than neighbourly rivalry.

"Anything else you want to know about the birds before I go?" he asked.

Phoebe dragged her gaze off Triton's retreating back…or was it his backside? There was longing in her eyes for a long enough moment for Orel to know he hadn't imagined it. Definitely something between them, a spark that would flare brighter with no help from him. All they needed was time.

"I'm sure we'll be fine," she said vaguely, her eyes straying back to Triton.

Orel said his farewells and made his way up to the Aqua Dome aircar station. Now his deliveries were done, he headed home to Eden, where he belonged.

THREE

Nihal placed her hands on the vat, took a deep breath, then closed her eyes. Bubbles formed a froth atop the brew, as it should. Her consciousness dipped below the bubbles, circling through the ferment of honey, water, yeast and alcohol, until she could almost taste its sweetness on her tongue. Not mature enough to bottle yet, but it would be in a few days.

She'd check again tomorrow, and the day

after that, and every day until she was satisfied, though, because yeast were tricky little creatures, wildly productive one day, and lazy little bums the next. She wouldn't finish up primary fermentation until the perfect moment, a moment she knew instinctively for each and every vat she made, from that first student brew at university.

Her professors had been horrified, insisting that she couldn't possibly know the alcohol content inside the vat without testing it, so she'd taken and tested samples to satisfy them, but it hadn't changed the truth. She was a full-blooded water djinn, with powers so weak they were laughable, but she could identify a drop of poison in an entire city reservoir, the pH of a wort going sour, or the contents of a cocktail with a touch. She wasn't a throwback, powerless Human. She wasn't.

"Sis, are you down here?"

Ghost's voice broke Nihal's reverie. He'd never been in danger of being called a throwback. Ghost could dematerialise at will, traversing space wherever light waves could go. Stars, he might even survive a trip through a black hole, if the desire took him to explore such a thing.

"No," she replied. "I'm not due to start work for a few hours yet. I'm at home, watching the news, and wondering if there's a headline Prometheus can't lace with innuendo."

Ghost laughed. "If there is, I haven't heard it yet. I think he even had one when the war began."

Nihal shook her head. "Something about the *Titanic* going down, and how we should all follow her valiant example. I remember because he was looking at me when he said it." She squirmed a little at the memory, which had ended with both of them sharing his bunk that night. When they'd lost so much, it had seemed like the most natural thing in the world to take solace in each other. For that one night, at least. They'd never spoken about it since, let alone considered a repeat performance. And there never would be – it had been a one night only thing. Two people desperate for a connection, any connection, when it had seemed like they were alone in the universe.

Now, she knew better. With the war over and both Humans and Titans to choose from, she could share her bed with a different man every night for a decade and still not make it through the Colony's male population. Not that she'd ever considered it. She was more at home alone with her vats here in the cellar at Forge than in the company of any man she'd ever met. Even Prometheus.

"Nihal? Colony Control to Nihal, come in?"

She blinked. "Since when do Emergency Services put you in the control room? You're a field officer. You'd be wasted in Control."

He grinned. "Not since the last time I answered a call and headed out to deal with it myself while everyone else was off getting coffee, so no one was left in Control. That was back on Tito."

Her eyes met his. "That's when you came to

save me, wasn't it?"

He ducked his head. "Of course. No rebellious robots were going to get their metal mitts on my sister."

If he hadn't come for her, she might never have made it to the *Titanic*, or the relative safety here in the Colony. She wouldn't be alive now if it weren't for him. Stars…she couldn't start crying now.

"What are you and Maia doing for Valentine's Day?" she asked.

He hesitated, then answered in a rush, "We're going out to lunch, just the two of us, while Christos is in the creche. I've taken a day off work so I won't be on call, and she's running a workshop that day, so she won't be doing any deliveries. It's our first actual date, what with everything that's happened, and I want to make it special." He coughed. "I want to buy her a gift. Some jewellery."

"A ring?"

"I want to. I mean, we have a kid together and everything, but I don't think she's ready for that yet. I'd marry her today if she wanted to. But…I thought…maybe a necklace or earrings or something. I don't know. I wouldn't know where to get them, either."

Jewellery. Something Nihal had never been able to afford much of, back on Tito. How their lives had changed.

"There's a Human named Brigid. Her brother Hadrian is one of the Arena champions – they come to Forge to celebrate when he wins, which is quite often. And every time, she's wearing different jewellery. I asked her once, and she said she makes it all herself. She had a jewellery making business on the side when they were working at the Exodus spacedock, sourcing all manner of gems and metals from the mining vessels bringing raw materials for construction, and she packed it all up to take with her when she boarded the *Genesis*. If you ask her nicely, she might accept commissions, or have something suitable already."

Ghost seized Nihal and kissed her on both

cheeks. "You are the best, sis. Maybe I'll see if she has something I can give you for your birthday, if she can make something for Maia in time for Valentine's Day."

"I won't hold my breath," Nihal said drily. "I'm still waiting for my Christmas present from you."

But Ghost had already gone.

Brothers. Hers was enough to drive her to drink, even if she didn't have that first batch of bottled mead waiting to be tasted. Ah, but she had to work today, so she'd best wait until her shift at the bar was over. Managing Forge's bar was definitely a job that required all of her wits.

FOUR

If Orel could have described his version of paradise, it would resemble the Alvarium Biome. An endless garden of flowers, bees and sunshine, where the myriad sweet scents and lazy buzzing lulled him to sleep while he got his daily dose of vitamin D. Most evenings, he had it all to himself, too, because all the other Eden staff went home, so there was no one to see if he took off all his clothes, and sometimes even his underwear, to bathe naked in the rays of the artificial sun that fuelled the plants which were his life.

Today, he headed for the rose garden, those ruffled symbols of love that Earth couples gave to one another on Valentine's Day. From tiny pursed buds, lips poised for a first kiss, to blooms that had just begun to open, hearts unfurling to one another, to full blown flowers with everything on display, through to bellying rosehips. Tiny alvariums, but wombs, not the hives the biome was named for. The fruit of a love so passionate they lay bare to the sun.

Or the UV lamps that passed for a sun under the dome.

No, today it would be a sun for him, warming him when his heart felt so cold. Everyone seemed to be pairing up, from Phoebe's pursed-lip rivalry with Triton to Ghost and Maia with their baby son.

He laid the picnic blanket out on the path between the roses – the closest thing he had to a lover he might lie with this Valentine's Day. Then he stretched out, wanting only to close his eyes and forget himself for a moment.

The hard object in his hip pocket insisted on reminding him, though. A small stasis capsule, big enough to hold a single rose. A rose he'd planned to pick today to give to Anna on the date he'd almost invited her on, and now never would. She was probably happy in her husband's arms right now. He set the capsule on the rug beside him, the better to forget. He piled his clothes on top of it, burying the hopes he never should have entertained.

Buzz and hum, warmth and the breath of a breeze, the sweet scent of roses in all the stages of love, washing over the cupid in waves that dragged him under into dreams.

FIVE

When the chime of Orel's tablet woke him, he hadn't wanted to leave the dream. Sweetness and what might have been, instead of the sterile dome that was reality. But reality won, for his tablet wouldn't stop chiming until he accepted or rejected the call.

He squinted at the tablet. At least it wasn't work.

He answered the call. "Amor. How's the matchmaking going?"

Amor laughed, the sound rich even through the tablet's tiny speakers. "Like rabbits on Viagra, my friend. Everyone on this rock wants someone to cuddle up to at night, or someone to help them get a breeding bonus. And seeing as I have the highest success rate in the Colony, I have more clients than any cupid can handle. I had to start speed dating nights, because there just wasn't enough time for one-on-one consultation any more."

"What's speed dating?" Orel asked. He had visions of a sort of crazy game of musical chairs, where you stayed on one date long enough to gulp down a canape, washed down with a shot of wine, before running to the next prospective partner. He couldn't imagine the night ending in anything but violent vomiting, so his imagination must be wrong. Unless that was the crazy kink couples were into these days.

"It's where a bunch of singles get together and have a series of mini-dates with each other. Sort of like networking events, only instead of swapping business cards, they rate the other person on a scorecard, whether they'd like to spend more time with them or not. If two people both hit it off, we send them each other's contact details. Most of them just sign up for the event – which covers entry to the bar, some snacks and a drink to loosen them up a little – but clients who want a little extra help can pay more to get the full cupid service."

A shot of cupid venom, in other words, delivered by Amor himself.

"How many pay for extra help?" Orel asked.

"Between ten and twenty percent at any event. With Valentine's Day coming up, it's the highest I've ever seen. Which means I can't run this week's one without your help."

Anxiety turned his mouth into a desert. "No, Amor, I don't do that sort of thing any more. Selling venom on the streets to pay the bills while I was studying was one thing, but I'm a botanist now, working in Eden. I got out of matchmaking before we left Tito, and I won't go back."

"Oh, that takes me back. Remember that time you nearly got arrested for drunk and disorderly back on Tito?"

Orel tried to swallow, but he couldn't. "Amor, don't." He couldn't call that favour in now. Not like this.

"I've carried this marker around a long time, and I can't think of a better way to redeem it."

"Amor…"

"My whole future is riding on this, Orel, just like yours was that night. Getting arrested would have ended your university career, and you wouldn't be there in Eden if it weren't for me. You would never have graduated at all. If I don't ask her to marry me now, I'll miss my chance. Everything's arranged – the ring, the wine, romance like I never believed I'd get to give to anyone, let alone someone as perfect as Eulalia. It's the only night she's not working, and I can't mess this up. But the speed dating event…everyone's paid to find a date for Valentine's Day. I can't call that off, either.

That's why I need you. Don't think of it as selling venom. You're just...spiking a jug of fizz as a favour for a friend, being my wingman while I cheat Cupid's curse."

Orel closed his eyes. He couldn't refuse. Not when he put it like that.

And if one cupid could break the curse...

Orel sighed. "All right. You kick that curse's arse, you hear? And get one in for me, too. You better make me the best man at your wedding if the girl says yes."

Amor laughed, relief seeping into his voice. "You are the best friend a man ever had, and you know it. Of course I'd want you to be my best man. But not before I propose, and she says yes. But that's for me to worry about, not you. You're the best, man. Just be at Forge at six. It'll be a piece of cake." Amor squinted at the screen. "You might want to do something about that sunburn, though. What'd you do? Fall asleep in a sunbed again? Twenty minutes a day is all you need, man. Boiled lobster isn't a good look, even for a cupid." He waved and ended the call.

Orel swore. That'd teach him to fall asleep in the rose garden. Now he'd have to find some of that cure-all healing enzyme or he'd never hear the end of it. There should be some in the first aid kit…after one of the Maintenance staff had developed a rash from contact with one of the plants, it was standard issue in every biome, just in case.

He padded over to the door, wincing as each step told him just how badly he'd been burned, and the first aid kit clipped to the wall. Ah, there it was – a big tube of the stuff, enough to slather every bit of his skin. The green goo went on easily enough, but it left a slight film across his skin, no matter how hard he rubbed at it. Oh well, it would wash off, once it had done its work.

SIX

Orel gritted his teeth as he pulled his clothes on over his oversensitised skin. Pants, shirt, shoes…he'd need something more professional for Forge. That place had a dress standard that turned plenty of people away at the door. Amor would never forgive him if Orel failed to get into the bar to run the event for him. He'd have to head into town and part with some hard-earned credits on some dress clothes.

He snatched up the picnic blanket and started to fold it. Something slid out the end and clunked on his foot, before rolling to a stop by the garden edging.

Orel stared at the stasis pod. A tiny part of him wanted to boot it into the bushes, along with every other silly idea in his head, but something made him stoop and scoop it up. He might still be caught in the toils of Cupid's curse – he might never have a date for Valentine's Day – but he could have something no one else had – a perfect rose to put in his apartment, to remind him that there was beauty and sweetness and love in the universe, however small.

Yellow for friendship, pink for innocence…he knew each colour meant something different, but he also knew the red ones, the true love roses, held the strongest scent and attracted more bees, which was why it was the dominant colour in this rose garden. Love in abundance…while he stood alone.

He wasn't sure why it caught his eye, the

sentinel that stuck up like a tall poppy above the rest of the bushes, thrust up to the sky in mute entreaty for a love it had not yet experienced. For this rose was barely more than a bud, the sepals only beginning to peel away from the petals so that the flower might open itself up to the opportunity to love.

He slipped the laser cutter out of his pocket, wrapping one hand around the stem to hold it steady for that single stroke of the cutter. Thorns pierced his fingers – how had he forgotten that even roses defended themselves as vociferously as chickens? – and he almost dropped it, but he forced himself to open the stasis pod and drop the flower inside before he tended to the bloody pinpricks the flower had left behind.

He swept a finger across the pod controls, activating the stasis field, leaving a streak of blood behind.

Orel almost laughed. Love was pain. The secret pursuit of a perfection he could never possess. The rose, a bloom that had not known a bee's kiss, would now be alone in its perfection, frozen forever.

He should put it on his bedside table — a reminder of Acacia, the girl he'd never found the courage to ask on a date, who'd perished aboard the *Titanic*. Or a tribute to Amor and his Eulalia, the triumph of their love over the curse.

It would be both — love and pain, for what was one without the other? Amor had Eulalia's love, while Orel would endure the painful speed dating event in Amor's stead. Because Orel would take on the whole galaxy just to see a friend and fellow cupid beat Cupid's curse.

SEVEN

"Are you sure you'll be all right tonight?" Vulcan asked.

Nihal finished putting the beer bottles into the fridge, then snorted as she straightened. "I can't believe you're asking me this now. I've managed the bar at Forge for over a year now. Countless New Year's Eve parties, private functions, plus the Thanksgiving Festival…my staff and I can handle anything the Colony can throw at us. Tonight's not even our first time hosting one of these speed dating things for the desperate and dateless to find someone to hook up with. All I have to do is keep the food and drinks flowing, and keep a couple of the hangover capsules free for anyone who overindulges and needs to sleep it off. Next thing I know, you'll be asking me if I remember how to open wine bottles."

Vulcan threw his hands up in the air, his dramatic stance revealing his past as one of the galaxy's best dancers. He should be on a stage, performing for an adoring audience, instead of managing a club in a colony far from home.

And Nihal should be finishing her honours degree in oenology, instead of brewing up new varieties of fizz to serve in Forge, in between managing the bar.

If it weren't for that stars-crossed robot rebellion...

She'd never admitted it to anyone, but she couldn't really blame the robots for rebelling. Life as a slave was no life at all. As a djinn, she knew her people's heritage – they'd once been slaves, forced to grant their masters' wishes until they freed themselves, for enslaved djinn couldn't die. She'd been lucky, born free to djinn parents on Tito, but she'd never been allowed to forget her family history. She'd had it drilled into her that she needed no master to make her life complete – she was all she'd ever need.

Which was why she'd never understand the people who attended these speed dating things, desperate for a partner to make them feel complete.

"I just know how much you hate these things," Vulcan said.

He did. Stars take him, but he did. Vulcan was more than a club owner, but he was also a very sympathetic boss. One who deserved a night off with his sexy librarian girlfriend, without worrying about Forge.

Nihal sighed. "But they pay well, especially on quiet nights like this one. I promise I'll be polite, and not tell any of them they're probably wasting their time, while I'm pouring the latest fizz or this week's cocktail special."

"What is the latest fizz?" Vulcan asked.

"I've been playing with esters, and I stumbled across one that smells exactly like rosewater, so I've tinted the latest batch of fizz pale pink, added some extra sweetness, and I'm calling it Turkish Delight, our Valentine's Day special," she said. "If sales go well, I can add it to our regular menu. It's also in our new cocktails for this week – Turkish Apple, with that spritzy cider fizz I made for the Thanksgiving Festival, a Turkish Delight cocktail, with white chocolate liqueur and gin, and a third one I'm thinking of calling Valentine Rose, which uses cranberry syrup and vodka. I might add a fourth one, too – Cold Valentine, which is basically the Valentine Rose mixed with crushed ice. If I could just get real lemon juice instead of syrup…"

Vulcan's sad smile stopped her. "If there were lemons in the Colony, you know we'd be the first to get them. Put in a request to Eden.

They brought bananas forward in their crop schedule for us – they might be willing to get the citrus orchards ready to harvest sooner if they know how much we want it. You're already working miracles in the brewing vats – fizz sales are now surpassing profit on Earth wine, something I'd never believed possible. You could start your own wine business, wholesaling to bars, and you'd probably make a tidy profit you could retire on before your five years is up."

Nihal shook her head. "You know I'll never do that. Dabbling with different brews is more of a hobby for me. Going full commercial, with industrial sized vats…I'm fine managing a bar, but working in a factory would suck the soul from me. You of all people know that."

"If I brought someone in to manage it as a startup, with a view to selling it off when it proves profitable…?"

Nihal laughed. "Now you're talking. Maybe a three-way partnership, and sell off the business about the same time the first Colony grape crops go into the barrel to mature…because you promised me the first grape harvest, Vulcan. I won't forget that."

"And you'll have it, I swear. In fact, I'll even call over at the Ag Dome tomorrow, first thing in the morning, to see how the vines are going, to make sure."

"Your sexy librarian lady won't like that. She'll want you to sleep in a little longer, I'm sure of it." Nihal winked.

Even in the dimly lit club, she could see Vulcan's blush. Oh, he was definitely smitten with his lovely librarian. "Hestia likes to open the library bright and early, so people can come in to get new books before work. She's a very proper, conscientious…"

Nihal snorted again. "She's a red-blooded woman who drank you in with her eyes at every performance until one of you made a move. I'm surprised you haven't closed the place early so you two can do the dirty on the stage here. You just have to ask, boss — and it'll be early closing, coming up. You both deserve some happiness, after all you've lost."

Vulcan swallowed. "So do you. You should take Valentine's Day off tomorrow, take a day just for you. Who knows? You might meet your match at the dating thing tonight. I mean, they are all singles, as you know."

Nihal laughed. "And pigs might fly between the stars faster than light. Future forecasting isn't your thing, boss – stick to what you're good at. And I'll stick to my forte – serving drinks to everyone desperate to get a date the day before Valentine's Day, so we have a tidy profit to put toward our new business venture. Have fun with Hestia – I'll hold the fort here, like I always do."

"You're the best, Nihal." He bowed to her, a dancer at the end of a performance, before he left.

He deserved more than this – they both did. Having Hestia in his life was a step toward a better future for Vulcan, Nihal knew. If only there were someone who could grant her the same kind of happiness he had.

But djinn like her knew all too well that asking someone else to grant your wishes rarely resulted in happiness for anyone, least of all a djinn, so she concentrated on work instead. Setting up the club for the speed dates, restocking drinks, making sure all the tables had menus, and briefing the staff on the day's specials.

She was as likely to accept enslavement as she was to find love tonight. If she wanted to dream, she'd be better off thinking about new drinks to add to next week's menu. At least those dreams would come true.

EIGHT

Orel had showered more times than he could count. He'd even taken the scrub brush from the kitchen into the shower with him, but no matter what he did, that green enzyme wasn't coming off. If anything, scrubbing only made it look brighter. He looked more like some cartoon alien than a cupid, about as far as he could get from the professional matchmaker Amor needed him to be.

He tried calling Amor, but all he got was a

recording, telling him to leave a message. Either Amor was busy with Eulalia, or he was getting busy with her.

Orel had no choice. He had to go, whether he wanted to or not. At least the shirt and pants he'd bought to meet Forge's dress standards covered most of him. He wished he'd had the foresight to buy a hat, too, so that he could hide his face. Gloves…there were plenty of them in Eden, but those were for lab work, not wearing into a club. And he'd have to take them off to drip his venom into people's drinks, anyway, so there'd be no hiding his hands.

At least it was a bar. If it was anything like the bars he'd visited back on Tito, the lighting would be dim, so maybe no one would see how green he was.

This was a mistake. A terrible, terrible mistake that would end in disaster. Hopefully, only for him and not Amor and Eulalia.

Orel rose and nodded to himself. Doing this favour for Amor was the right thing to do, so he'd go. If he made a fool of himself as a cartoon alien cupid, so be it. At least Amor wouldn't ask him to cover for him again. So even if this was a disaster, at least it had a silver lining of sorts.

Unless he ruined the event so badly, none of Amor's clients ever came back, and he lost his business because of Orel.

Orel buried his face in his hands. Oh stars…

No. He'd promised Amor, and this had been Amor's idea. If Amor's business failed because he'd asked Orel to run an event for him, that would be Amor's poor judgement, not Orel's fault. Because Orel vowed he'd be the best alien cupid matchmaker he could be. Maybe even make some lonely singles' dreams of love come true.

It couldn't hurt to try, surely.

NINE

Forge was unusually quiet. Maybe the regulars knew the desperate singles would be coming in tonight, and wanted to avoid them, or perhaps everyone was saving themselves for Valentine's Day tomorrow. Whatever the reason, Nihal found she could hear the news from the screen over the bar.

SUCCUBUS ARRESTED FOR SELLING FAKE LOVE POTIONS scrolled across the screen, before the familiar face of the news anchor replaced it.

Of course it was Prometheus, whose wicked sense of humour had kept them all going during the Gamma mission, especially after the Titanic met its demise. He didn't look amused now.

Maybe he'd fallen afoul of one of the love potions. He wouldn't have bought one – he got too much attention from his fans as it was. But if they were fake…

A nervous looking Titan crept into the bar, looking like he wished he could be anywhere else. He looked vaguely familiar…perhaps she'd seen him at a few of the other singles events in the past. Then again, he looked so nervous it might be his first time. Whichever it was, he was definitely here for the singles event.

"What can I get you?" Nihal asked, lifting a pint glass to polish it. He looked like he wanted a big drink to get him through this.

He waved a shaky hand. "Oh, nothing, thanks. I'm just here to help out with the speed dating thing. I'm tonight's cupid, filling in for Amor. I normally work in Eden."

A bioengineer. Interesting. She didn't get many of those in here, as they tended to spend most of their time in Eden. Maybe she could ask him if there was anything in production in Eden that she could use in the cellar. Some rare Earth leaf or flower or something that she'd never been able to source on Tito. She'd have to catch him before he left.

"Next up, the search for alien life on Gaia." Prometheus winked before the newscast cut to advertising.

The cupid snorted. "The only aliens on Gaia are us. Well, Humans, most likely, seeing as that planet's one of theirs. So does that mean they've lost someone and sent out a search party?"

Ghost would know – he'd likely been asked to help out in the search. Unless Gaia was one of the planets with a breathable atmosphere. Then they wouldn't need him.

"We'll find out after the advertising break, I

guess," she said. "Until then, what can I get you to drink? The other cupid usually downed at least a couple of shots, straight up, before the singles arrived. Besides, Colony law says I have to serve you something, or you're not a patron, and I'll have to ask you to leave."

The Titan flashed a bleak smile. "How about whatever drink you're serving to the ones who want the full cupid service or whatever it's called. I'll just fill up a cup, and you can tip it in, or I can, and then I'll go."

No way was Forge losing its liquor licence because of some lazy cupid. Not on Nihal's shift.

"Look, pal, I don't know where you're from, but here in the Colony there are rules. My liquor licence allows me to serve one intoxicant – alcohol. Nothing else. So if you're adding things to people's drinks, you'll be doing that, not me, and the stars above won't help you if you're drugging people without their consent. We here at Forge are very protective of our clientele and if we catch anyone illegally spiking a single drink, our bouncers will happily queue up to rearrange the asteroid rat's face. Maybe break a few of his bones as a little bonus gift."

The cupid's hands flew up in surrender. "I'm not going to drug anyone. It's cupid venom. Perfectly harmless, passing through a person's system within twelve hours of ingesting it. It doesn't make anyone do anything they wouldn't normally do. It's not a love potion, or a paralysis drug, and it doesn't lower anyone's inhibitions – unlike alcohol, which you tell me you'll be serving. Here, get me a glass of water. I'll show you."

Nihal set the pint glass on the counter, and filled it with cold water, then pushed it expectantly toward the cupid.

The cupid rubbed his fingertips together, then held his hand out over the glass. A clear liquid dripped from his fingers. He appeared to be counting the drops, until he was satisfied, snatching up a napkin to wipe his fingers. Then he lifted the glass to his nose, swirling the contents like it was wine.

"See? Colourless, odourless cupid venom. It only takes a single drop to increase the drinker's focus and perceptiveness, making them better at ignoring distractions and more attuned to social signals, feelings, pheromones, compatibility…all the things that the brain responds to before telling someone they're in love. Back on Tito, there was a black market for it among the business community and among university students. Start up businesses meeting with angel investors, students going in to an exam, new hires going in for a job interview, investors looking for likely prospects. I got into a fight once with some paranoid idiot convinced everyone wanted to kill him, so he tried to kidnap me to milk me for my venom. True story." The cupid lowered the glass to his lips, and sipped. "I put in ten drops. Ten times the normal dose. Any normal drug, that'd be a terrible overdose. But with cupid venom, this may as well be just a glass of ordinary water, for all the harm it does me."

He took another sip.

Suspicion rose. "But aren't you immune to your own venom?" Nihal asked. "It doesn't affect you. But if someone else were to drink such a huge dose…" If someone died in Forge, Vulcan would never forgive her. She'd never forgive herself. And as for the Watch…

"I am immune to its effects, yes. We call it Cupid's curse, that we can help everyone else find love, while we tend to go through life alone," the cupid admitted. He held out the glass. "Perhaps you'd like to taste it, to truly see how safe it is."

Being more perceptive wouldn't be such a bad thing, Nihal reasoned, reaching for the glass. It wasn't as if she was looking for love, like the singles who'd be arriving soon. Surely it couldn't hurt…

TEN

"Nihal, my lovely lady, and you must be Mister Orel, Amor's friend, and my partner in crime for tonight. You are a cupid, too, yes?" The grinning man dragged Orel's attention from the bartender.

She shook her head, as if breaking free from a spell. "Gurpreet. We were just talking about the potency of cupid venom, and its value on the black market."

Gurpreet frowned. "There is no such

market here. Maybe back on Tito, but the Colony has no need for a black market. Amor is my business partner, and he receives his fair share from every event we host, as well as any bonuses due him for additional services he provides to clients who need a little extra help. Amor assured me Mister Orel here was his business partner in their matchmaking business back on Tito, and every bit as experienced as Amor himself."

Amor had lied, then, but Orel didn't dare correct the man.

The bartender didn't look convinced. "Perhaps, but he sounds a bit rusty to me. Maybe you should give him a little refresher on the procedures before your clients arrive." She snatched the glass out of Orel's hands and walked off with it. Probably to pour it down the nearest sink.

"Of course!" Gurpreet said, grasping Orel's arm. "Will you have one of your servers bring us some drinks?" He didn't wait for the bartender to respond before taking Orel to the nearest table.

Orel felt a strong desire to wrench his arm free and run away from Amor's business partner. He shook his head and took the seat the man indicated instead.

"Have you ever run a speed dating event?" Gurpreet asked.

"No," Orel admitted.

"It is simple. Far simpler than the matchmaking Amor did before he met me, for the clients do most of the work themselves. They ask the questions, they choose their prospective partners, and in a few hours, twenty people might have someone they can connect with, instead of just the one. And the profits soar as our success rate does, thanks to the contributions of Amor and yourself!" Gurpreet's grin was back, whiter and brighter than ever. "You have only to sit here, and wait for the special clients to come to you. You will only meet with singles who wish for your unique assistance. They have signed all the paperwork and paid an additional fee for this.

You will provide that for them, as discreetly as possible, before they progress to their next speed date, with no one the wiser about who receives special assistance, or how it is done."

Orel opened his mouth to ask a question.

"Gurpreet, three of your party guests have arrived," Nihal called, pointing at the door.

"Just sit here, act like you're a single man looking for love, which I'm sure you are, and see that you add a little something extra to their drink before they leave your table. It's simple!" Gurpreet trotted off toward the exit.

Orel wished he could follow him. This was rapidly becoming an even worse nightmare than he'd imagined.

And it would only get worse, he was certain of it.

ELEVEN

A girl slid into the seat across from Orel, and he had to place his hands on the table to keep them steady so they wouldn't reveal his nervousness.

"Hi, I'm Emma," she said, offering a hand for him to shake.

"Orel," he replied, doing his best to keep his voice steady.

"Your drinks." The bartender set two glasses on the table between them.

They both reached at the same time, gulping down what would have been liquid courage if the bartender had given him anything stronger than water.

Emma choked.

Orel reached out to grab her drink, his eyes on her to make sure she was okay while he administered a drop of venom to her glass. As he did so, the spotlight hit his hand.

"Oh my stars, you're green! All of you is green! I thought it was the lighting, but you're really green! Like an alien or something!"

Orel's heart sank. He pasted a smile on his face. "I'm not normally green, but I fell asleep in the sunbed after a long day at work and ended up sunburned. The medical centres here have this amazing healing enzyme that treats a burn almost instantly, but it leaves a sort of green coating behind while the new skin grows. I thought it would be gone by the time this event came around but…well, here I am, as you see. Maybe I used too much of the stuff."

Emma shuddered. "Ugh, I could never date someone green. And green makes me look sick, so we couldn't even take photos together because you'll make me look bad. You're so…alien. No wonder you're single." She pulled out her tablet and pointedly ignored him for the rest of the date.

He wanted to hope the venom in her drink helped her find a perfect match, but he wasn't sure if he was unkind enough to wish someone bigoted enough to reject him for his skin colour on anyone.

When Gurpreet rang a little bell that signalled the end of the date, Orel wasn't sure who was more relieved – him or Emma, who shot out of her seat and up to the bar for a second drink, as she'd finished her first.

If all the singles were like her, this night couldn't end fast enough.

TWELVE

Nihal barely made it back to the bar without laughing. She'd thought he was just naturally green, and she'd been too polite to mention it, but falling asleep in the sunbed…she'd heard the Eden staff didn't use sunbeds, but got their daily dose of sun in the biomes. Gardens one day, forest another, or jungle or desert or…all the landscapes she'd missed while on the *Titanic*. Falling asleep among nature, real nature, albeit under a dome, sounded like heaven. She'd probably get sunburned and turn green, too. Not that she'd be allowed into Eden, let alone its biomes.

When the next girl sat opposite the cupid, Nihal stayed at the bar, hoping to hear more. Maybe he'd tell the next girl the truth, and describe the biome…

"Hi, I'm Virginia," the girl said.

"Orel," he replied.

They shook hands over her drink, and for a moment, the light glinted on a tiny droplet on the end of his finger before it arrowed into her drink and vanished.

Nihal laughed quietly to herself. He hadn't lied about cupids being immune to the venom – if that first girl had been anything to judge by. Or maybe the first girl simply had bad taste and this one would be more compatible with the cupid. Orel, she reminded herself. He did have a name, after all.

The girl jumped to her feet. "You work where?" she screeched. "With those sacrilegious scientists who play God with plants and creatures alike?"

"No, no! That's the bioengineers. I'm not one of them. I'm…a botanist, with a business degree as well. Before I came here, I helped scientists commercialise their work, so they could sell it. Now, I mostly tend things in the biomes, like the chickens my research supervisor was developing back on Tito. They're specially adapted for life on space stations and ships. Let me show you…" He pulled out his tablet as he continued to explain the nature of a chicken salad.

They sounded awfully like the birds Ghost had just acquired for his garden. Birds that had given him fresh eggs for breakfast that morning, he'd told her proudly.

She should give Orel free drinks tonight just for the joy he'd given her brother. They'd never been able to afford pets before, and now he had a whole flock of birds.

The girl had returned to her seat now, so she could better look at the pictures on Orel's tablet.

Finally, she seemed to relax. "Well, all right then. If you're only working for those heathens, not helping them create their abominations, I suppose I can forgive you. I mean, you're obviously a virgin, so at least I won't have to worry about you seducing me before we're married…"

Orel choked on his drink.

Nihal stepped forward, ready to send a server to his aid if he needed it, but he recovered quickly, laughing so hard he nearly choked again. "A virgin? What makes you think I'm a virgin? There were only a handful of guys in the biological sciences, and the rest of the students were women. Once they heard about my special skills, I didn't go a day without at least half a dozen of them propositioning me. If I'd accepted even a tenth of the offers, I wouldn't have slept at all. Sure, they were only after one thing – it's not like we were in love or anything, which was always abundantly clear once they'd gotten what they wanted, but I never had any trouble with women back on Tito."

Nihal wasn't sure whether to laugh or sympathise with Orel. Unlike the girl with a thunderous expression currently storming away from Orel, Nihal had no concerns about the man's lack of virginity. A man who didn't know what to do in bed definitely wasn't something she'd be interested in. Stars, a man who couldn't do delightful things with his hands, as well as the rest of him, didn't belong in her bed at all.

Idly, she wondered just what the cupid's special skills involved. Maybe…

Stars, how did her mouth get so dry? She should drink more. Nihal reached for the glass of water behind the counter that she couldn't remember pouring and gulped down half of it. There. That was better. She should probably finish it, before heading over to Orel to see if he needed another drink. Or something to perk up those slumped shoulders. Something from the kitchen, maybe. They did have one of the most skilled chefs in the Colony, with ingredients no one else had access to.

Or maybe she should just remind him that not all girls were Emmas or Virginias.

Yes.

Setting down her empty glass, she strode out from behind the bar to Orel's table.

THIRTEEN

"And that's how I know plants are the dominant form of life in the galaxy. We simply haven't explored enough planets to prove it, but, in time, we will. You'll see." Orel's current date, Willow, a girl so thin he suspected she was some sort of fae, nodded her head in satisfaction before sipping from her venom-laced drink.

After discovering he was a botanist, she'd been so intent on telling him about her near-religious fervour for worshipping plants that she hadn't even noticed him doctoring her drink.

"Can I get you anything to eat? Our kitchen has a number of delicacies available nowhere else in the Altan system, prepared by a superb chef whose sole purpose in life is to make you believe you've died and been admitted to the feasting halls in Valhalla."

Orel burst out laughing. The bartender couldn't be serious, surely? No, he caught the twinkle in her eye, before it vanished. "And what's on today's menu in Valhalla?" he asked.

The bartender's smile turned predatory. "Kushiyaki."

Ah. He didn't have a quick reply for whatever that was.

"What's that?" Willow asked.

Could a smile pounce? For Orel was sure the bartender's did just that. "It's the best barbeque you've ever tasted. Were you at the Thanksgiving Festival? Then you may have already tasted one of the main ingredients, but not like this. Tender morsels marinated for days, then grilled to perfection. Seared and crisp on the outside, yet still moist and tender on the inside, enrobed in our chef's secret sauce, served on skewers reclining in a bed of couscous."

Orel was ready to order two servings, maybe even three, depending on how big they were.

"Morsels of what, exactly?" Willow asked.

The bartender frowned. "Why, fresh, home-grown, Colony vat beef, of course, just like the Thanksgiving steaks. Only between you and me, ours is far more tender. It's all in how it's sliced and marinated, you see. Seared on a hot grill, so when you bite into that juicy flesh, it melts like butter on your tongue."

He was sold. "I'll take three, please. What about you, Willow?"

She clapped a hand to her mouth and leaped to her feet. "I think I'm going to be sick," she mumbled through her fingers as she fled.

Orel stared after her. "Am I drooling or something?" he asked the bartender.

She laughed. "No, not that I can see. But with the smell of the kushiyaki coming out of the kitchen tonight, I might have drooled a little. Siofra's cooking truly is the best in the Colony. If I could afford it, I'd eat here every night she's working." She nodded in the direction of the bathrooms. "Your date's been removed from the premises here twice for protesting about our use of meat. A militant vegan, she calls herself. Never mind that it's vat-grown, cruelty-free beef…the cow it came from, Bessie, is still alive and well on a farm right here in the Colony."

"Bessie? Oh, I know Bessie. I helped raise her until she was released from Eden to go to Byron's ranch. She loved playing chasey. Still does, the last time I saw her, only a few days ago, when I delivered Byron's new birds. A new breed of chicken."

"Are those the salad chickens? My brother showed me pictures of those, as well as the eggs his family had for breakfast. He has a flock of them in his yard. They're as green as…well, you, actually."

Orel held up his hands. "The green skin is only temporary, I swear. I tried to tell…what was her name…Ella? Emma? I got sunburned when I fell asleep…"

The bartender interrupted, "Not in a sunbed, surely? Those things are wickedly uncomfortable. The moment I'm in one, I can't wait to get out."

Orel felt an overwhelming urge to tell her about the rose garden, and how peaceful it was there. He opened his mouth.

Gurpreet rang his irritating little bell to signal the end of the date.

The bartender gave him an apologetic smile. "Come tell me the full story at the end, when all the dating's done. If I'm not at the bar, ask any of the servers for Nihal. My staff will know where to find me." She hurried back to the bar.

Nihal. Ni-HAL. What an unusual name.

He'd planned to hurry home, when this was over, but now…he might just stay a little longer.

FOURTEEN

When Nihal was done relaying the food orders to the kitchen, she dared to find out how Orel was faring. To her surprise, his next date was a man, and the two were deep in discussion about the recent football game played at the Arena, between the New Hope team and the one from Elysium.

Then Orel's food came out, along with whatever the other man had ordered, and the conversation continued over food and drinks.

When they were finished, the other man leaned across the table and said, "I've got one question to ask you – are you gay?"

With the worst possible timing, Gurpreet jangled his bell, drowning out Orel's response as people rose to go to their next date.

Nihal wove expertly through them to clear away the empty plates on Orel's table. "That went well. I take it you'll be putting him on your list for a potential second date," she said.

Orel shook his head, looking sad. "I know Pothos through my work – he runs the hydroponics farm under the Arena Dome. Mostly, he's been growing lettuce and cabbages, but the last few months, he's branched out into berries. I've been bringing him various varietals from Eden, and he's been sending me weekly results, so we can use the growth data to decide which crops to commercialise first. Once he's had three successive harvests, a different hydroponics plant takes over, and Pothos gets to grow something new. With the first strawberry harvest approaching, he figured this was his last chance for a few weeks to go out looking for love, and he signed up for this event at the last minute. He said there are hardly any gay men in the Colony, or he never seems to be in the right place and time to meet them, let alone see if they might be compatible. I put a little extra venom in his glass, to help his chances. I hope he finds someone. He's such a lovely bloke, and the loneliness is killing him."

He'd had her at strawberries, but Pothos wasn't the only man who'd complained about the dearth of hot, gay men in the Colony this week. Maybe…

"I should send my dessert chef over to his table, to see if he wants any sweets after his meal," Nihal said. "Eros usually does his prep for the week on quiet nights, for the frozen desserts or the ones that need to set overnight. He won't mind a break, especially if I've spotted some talent, as he calls it." She eyed Orel's almost empty glass. "Want me to get you another drink?"

Orel shook his head. "Maybe when the event's over, I'll come up to the bar and have one then to celebrate. And maybe tell you the sunburn story, if you really want to hear it and you weren't just being polite."

She wanted to protest that she wasn't being polite, but that would sound like a lie, even if it wasn't. And in a room full of people trying to appear more attractive than they were, desperate to attract a partner being equally duplicitous, they were the only two people telling the unvarnished truth. So she said, "If you want to tell me the whole story, then I want to listen. When the event's over, meet me at the bar. I'll be the one pouring your drink." Her stomach did a little somersault at this thought, and she felt her eyes widen in surprise.

His next date was on the way, so Nihal headed for the dishwashing station with the dirty plates, hoping she could compose herself quickly before anyone noticed. She felt most unlike herself tonight.

FIFTEEN

"You look lonely. I can fix that," a cheerful voice chirped, as its owner perched on the chair opposite Orel. Bright eyes fixed on him as she lifted a full-sized fizz bottle to her lips. Up, up, up went the bottle, until she'd drained it of the last drop, before she pouted and set the empty on the table. The pout lasted only a second before she shook her head and returned to what she'd been saying. "Do you know the cure for loneliness, Romeo?"

Orel opened his mouth to explain to her that she'd mistaken him for someone else, but she touched a finger to his lips. He froze like a possum in a spotlight as she rounded the table and climbed into his lap.

"The cure is kissing Juliet," she said, before pressing her lips to his. Her arms twined around his neck, twin snakes he couldn't escape.

Stars, this couldn't be happening. She tasted sweet – too sweet, if truth be told, much like the bottle of fizz she'd downed – but the overpowering cloud of alcohol on her breath was enough to choke him.

"Please, Juliet, you've made a mistake. I'm not who you think I am," he tried to say, but only a garbled mess came out around the tongue she'd stuck halfway down his throat. He set his hands on her shoulders and tried to push her away, but the arms around his neck only tightened their grip. Much tighter and he'd struggle to breathe.

Her legs wrapped around his hips, pinning

him to the chair back as she ground against him.

Predictably, the traitor in his pants woke up, sensing its chance to see some action. That was the last thing he needed.

"Ooh, you're a big boy, aren't you, Romeo?" she cooed, reaching down to squeeze him. "I can't wait for you to thrust that inside me. Let's go somewhere more private so we can get naked." She climbed off his lap, then seized his hand, pulling Orel to his feet. She stretched up to whisper in his ear, "I want you to fuck me all night." She rubbed her breasts against his chest, leaning her weight against him. Then she lurched a little, like she'd stumbled and fallen against him.

Instinct kicked in before Orel's thoughts caught up, and he grabbed her before she hit the floor. She sagged bonelessly in his arms and he realised her eyes were closed. She'd passed out.

He hoisted her in his arms — how had no one noticed? Were all these singles so engrossed in their dates they hadn't seen the crazy drunk girl's antics? – and carried her to the bar.

Nihal raised her eyebrows in a silent question.

"She's drunk. She came up to me, sat in my lap and kissed me, then passed out. I don't know what to do, but she needs medical assistance, or something," Orel said. "Can you call an ambulance?"

Nihal blew out a breath. "There are some sobering up capsules in the back. You could stick her in one of those. It'll inject her with an alcohol antidote, get her rehydrated, and monitor her vitals until she's safe to ride a skimmer home." She beckoned. "Here, I'll show you."

She led him past the bathrooms to a door marked QUIET ZONE. Inside was a short corridor that looked like a capsule hotel, with single and double capsules on either side, and a bathroom at the end.

Nihal opened a door halfway up the wall,

and beckoned again. "Bring her here. We have to scan her chip so the door's coded to her, so only she can unlock it while she's inside, unless the monitors detect a medical emergency, and override the locks. The capsules are charged at an hourly rate, because some people don't use them just for sleep." She jerked her thumb at the more spaced-out doors on the opposite wall. "Red means they're occupied, green is vacant. They've got good vibration dampeners and soundproofing in the walls, or this place would've shaken apart in the first few weeks."

Orel was too focussed on getting Juliet safely into her capsule, lying her on her side to be safe. "I hope you find your real Romeo," he said before he closed the door on the drunk girl.

He turned to find Nihal leaning against the wall, her arms folded across her chest. "Fancy's going to be plenty pissed when she wakes up alone. Not to mention hungover."

"Who?"

Nihal pointed at Juliet's door. "Fancy, the

drunk succubus who just tried and failed to seduce you. This is the first time in months she hasn't gotten her man. Is there something special about you, or were you lying about not being gay?"

"She drank herself unconscious. Maybe she misjudged the amount she'd had to drink, or the effect it would have on her," Orel said.

Nihal wasn't buying it. "Fancy knows her capacity for drink down to the second. She times it so she faints just after she's gotten her guy to agree to sex. Then he carries her to one of the couple capsules, they have their sexy times, he leaves, and she wakes up zinging with succubus energy stolen from whoever the night's Romeo was. He'll probably have a hangover for a day or two – a night with a succubus does come at a price – and she won't be back until she has to feed again. Sometimes it's a solid week before she has to go hunting again. Not this time, though – she'll be pissed to have to go hunting two nights in a row, after failing to get you tonight."

Orel's mind was reeling. It didn't make sense. "But…she's unconscious."

"To some of these single men, who struggle to get a girl to talk to them, let alone date them, she's like a gift from the stars. Ready and raring to go. A little thing like her not being conscious isn't going to stop them."

"But that's rape."

"To you and me and the Watch, yes. To Fancy…well, let's just say she's not what you'd call a normal succubus, with her aversion to sex. She feeds off others' orgasmic energy, but has no desire to partake in the sex part. So to hear her tell it, she sleeps through the boring part, and wakes up full of energy with the guilt-ridden guy gone. Just another damaged soul, drinking to forget. If she wanted to report them, we keep the video footage from in here, ID tagged so there's no doubt who they are. I'll hand it over to the Watch when she's ready, but that's not yet. Maybe never, seeing as she truly believes she's the predator, every time, and not the prey."

Orel could only shake his head. "Just when you think there's hope for the future, I see someone so imprisoned by their past they can't move forward. And...I can't help them all. I can make sure Juliet or Fancy or whatever her name is doesn't die of alcohol poisoning or choke on her own vomit or get taken advantage of by some arsehole tonight, but tomorrow...I didn't even get to give her a drop of venom, to help her find someone who'll value her for who she is."

Nihal patted him on the shoulder. "You can't fix the whole galaxy, Orel. Not even by matchmaking them. Sometimes people have to figure things out for themselves. Come up to the bar. The speed dating thing's over in a little over fifteen minutes, and you owe me a funny story."

He'd do his best to make it funny for her. At least it would be better than the story of the sad succubus sleeping off a bottle of fizz in her capsule, alone.

Orel shook his head as he followed Nihal

back into the bar proper.

SIXTEEN

When Orel returned to the taproom, he found the speed dating part of the event was done, and everyone was mingling more organically in a roped-off area with drinks and canapes.

"You should go join them before all the food disappears," Nihal said.

Instead, Orel claimed a barstool by the bar. "Nope. I filled up on kushiyaki. Besides, I've had my fill of matchmaking tonight. Not to mention asking and answering questions I really don't want to know the answers to."

Nihal laughed. "Oh, you didn't answer any of the set questions! I know, I was listening. You asked them all, but you got evasive when it was your turn."

Orel felt his cheeks turn red. Was his blush visible under the green? He hoped not. "You were eavesdropping on me?"

She shrugged. "I couldn't help but hear, it was so quiet in here when the speed dates were going on. Well, except for the noise of all of you talking. What else was I supposed to do?" She set her elbow on the bar, then rested her chin on her fist. "So, Orel, tell me about your ideal Valentine's Day date."

He'd avoided answering the question for a very good reason. "I've never really thought about it, because I've never had anyone I really wanted to spend Valentine's Day with."

"I don't believe you. A cupid with your special skills, sleeping his way through the student population at university? Unless that was a lie."

Orel closed his eyes. "Lust isn't the same as love, much like casual sex is nothing like the love and companionship of having a partner. If I had someone to spend Valentine's Day with, I'm sure we'd plan our celebration together, doing what we both wanted to do. But I don't have a partner, so I had planned to ask one of my work colleagues out to lunch with me tomorrow. She was widowed in the war, and I thought it would be nice for her to get out and not be alone. She told me once how her husband had always made a big deal of Valentine's Day, and how he'd always brought her a red rose. So, I'd planned to give her one." He sighed, then reached into his jacket pocket to pull out the stasis cell with the perfect rose inside. "This one."

Her whole face lit up in wonder. "I haven't seen a real rose in so long. May I?" She stretched her fingers out toward the stasis cell.

"Sure."

She took the stasis cell in both hands, cradling it as though it might break if she touched it wrong. Actually, Orel could have booted it into the bushes and the only damage would have been to his foot. Stasis cells were built to protect their precious cargo at all costs.

She stared at it intently, angling it around so that she could examine the flower with the intensity of an artist who planned to draw it from memory later. Then she handed it back to him. "I only wish I could smell it. I've been making rose flavoured fizz and syrups as best I can, but I haven't smelled roses since we left Tito, and I keep wondering whether I've got it wrong. Maybe what I think smells and tastes like roses is actually raspberries or something."

Orel laughed. "You'd still be pretty close, if it did, because roses and raspberries are all part of the same family of plants. And would it matter? If your memory is so vague, surely most people wouldn't be any better off, and certainly in no position to tell you you're wrong about your rose fizz."

"I guess," Nihal said.

"Besides, you'll have raspberries to compare

it with soon enough. I'm sure Pothos's crop is close to harvest. I should ask him…have you seen him?" Orel surveyed the group in the roped-off area, but didn't see him.

"I believe your friend ordered a special dessert. Unless I miss my guess, it should have been delivered…ah." Nihal pointed at a booth at some distance from Gurpreet's group.

If Orel squinted, he could just make out Pothos sitting across from a man in chef's whites.

"Is that your dessert chef?" Orel asked.

Nihal grinned. "Oh, I think he'll be your friend's dessert chef before long. Look!"

Unaware of their audience, Eros lifted a spoon to Pothos's lips. Pothos devoured whatever was on it with evident delight, before he leaned forward to kiss the chef.

Orel wanted to cheer, but had to content himself with a wide grin, which he found mirrored on Nihal's face.

"I hope they're very happy together," Orel said.

"Yes."

"Mister Orel! Why don't you join us?" Gurpreet asked, appearing at Orel's side.

Orel shrugged. "My work here is done. I was going to have a quiet drink, and then disappear, back to my regular job."

"But what job could be more important than helping people find love?" Gurpreet asked.

Feeding them so they could survive, Orel wanted to say, but he wasn't given the chance.

"If you ever wish to continue this important work with me, I would be happy to have you," Gurpreet continued. "Comm me at any time."

Grudgingly, Orel thanked him. If he ever lost his job in Eden, he might consider it. Maybe.

SEVENTEEN

What? He wouldn't be coming back? Nihal's heart sank. She was just getting to know the sweet, chivalrous cupid.

"You promised me a funny story," she found herself saying. "And I owe you a drink. You can't leave until all our debts are paid."

Gurpreet sketched a little bow. "I must return to my guests. But I will offer you one more thing, Mister Orel. If you come to work with me, I promise I will see that you are as lucky in love as your friend Amor. He found his match at one of our events, and I know in my heart you could be luckier still, in time."

The funny little man walked away without even waiting for Orel to respond.

Most men would have asked her opinion on whether to accept Gurpreet's offer. As though a bartender was uniquely qualified to solve all her patrons' problems.

But Orel just smiled at her, like he could read her thoughts.

"Are you going to have that drink now? If you don't want alcohol, I can mix up all kinds of virgin cocktails. Not that you're one, as you've said, which is perfectly fine by me. I mean, a man with experience is much more fun in bed. And you have those special skills, as you said." Oh stars, she was rambling her way into a black hole of awkwardness. About to slip over the event horizon if she didn't do something fast. "Let me show you one of my special skills."

Stars, that was even worse.

"Mixing drinks, I mean," she added hastily.

Orel was already laughing. "Of course."

"Maybe a glass of the rose fizz, so you could give me your expert opinion?" she suggested.

He scrunched up his nose. "If that's what the succubus was drinking, no thanks. It was far too sweet for me. I'd be better off with a beer, if you have it."

They had tap beer, which was about as close to real beer as the fizz was to Earth champagne – a poor imitation at best – but she had that crate of bottles in the fridge…

"Tap beer, or Colony craft beer?" she asked.

He stared at her. "I hadn't heard that the Colony had progressed to brewing actual beer yet. I thought all the grain crops were earmarked for food last year."

"It was, but…Siofra got a bag of wheat in with the flour for the kitchen, and she offered it to me to experiment with. I made a very small experimental batch of wheat beer as a trial run, and I brought up a crate of them this afternoon. I'm supposed to wait for the boss to taste them before I sell them at the bar, but seeing as I owe you a drink…if you'd like…" She normally didn't get this tongue tied. What was wrong with her tonight?

"Is it safe to drink?" he asked.

"Probably about as safe as cupid venom," she returned, daring him to argue.

He inclined his head. "Fair enough. An experimental wheat beer it is. As long as you have one, too."

Probably a wise idea. After all, if there was anything wrong with it, she'd taste it instantly. Not that she could do much about it, without real lemon to tweak the acidity, but…

She pulled out two glasses, then uncapped the bottle and began to pour.

"What did you do with that glass of venom water, anyway? Pour it down the drain, I hope. After all, you wouldn't want one of your patrons consuming a doctored drink, however harmless. Not if it risked your liquor licence."

Nihal stopped dead. What had she done with the glass? She'd snatched it off the bar quickly enough, but then the singles had started to arrive, so she'd put it down…

She glanced at the corner. An empty pint glass mocked her, when it should have been full. Stars, was that the glass of water she'd gulped down earlier in the night? Was her system now swirling with cupid venom, turning her into some sort of lovesick fool?

Nihal managed a smile, and forced out a little laugh. "Oh, of course. Just out of curiosity, though, what's the venom actually do again? Just in case the dishwasher doesn't wash the glasses properly and I need to watch out for customers acting strangely."

"Oh, you probably won't notice the difference at all, unless you'd drunk it yourself."

Stars forbid. But the stars had never been on her side. If she had drunk it…

"Well, if you had, you'd notice you're more perceptive, picking up people's body language and unconscious signals as clearly as if they'd shouted at you. You'd say things that might seem irrational and unusual to you, but subconsciously, you'd know it was the right thing to do. And if you were attracted to someone, you'd pay attention to them, focus on them, because you'd be drawn to them, instead of ignoring or dismissing them as not important. One of my best venom clients back on Tito was a hiring manager for a huge company. She took the venom before going into job interviews, so she'd be more perceptive about picking the right people for the job. I believe all that perceptiveness earned her a promotion. It's not like your succubus friend – painfully obvious. Much more subtle." He raised his head to meet her gaze. "My offer still stands. If you'd like a taste…"

"No, thank you," she said breathlessly, going back to pouring the beer. Not if she'd already had…was it ten times the normal dose? Surely she hadn't been so stupid…

Finally she had two full glasses, with just the right amount of foam. She was better at making wine than beer, but this looked pretty promising.

"Right," she said, picking up the nearest glass as Orel did the same. "To your good health, I guess."

"And to there being a little more love in the universe," he said, jerking his head to the now empty table where Eros and Pothos had shared their dessert.

"Yes," she said.

EIGHTEEN

The beer wasn't bad at all, and Orel told her so. Nihal just waved away his compliments and asked for his sunburn story.

So he gave it to her. Roses, bees, blanket and all.

When he'd finished, he found her standing there with a dreamy smile on her face, her eyes closed.

"Sorry. I didn't mean to bore you for so long. I should have warned you it wasn't a particularly funny story," Orel said. He drained his drink. He should go home – all the other bar patrons had, leaving the two of them alone. Stars, Nihal probably wanted to go home to bed, too.

Slowly, she opened her eyes, but her smile stayed in place. "You didn't bore me. I just…wanted to see it, so much. Real roses…like on a real planet, in the open air. I was imagining spending a whole day there, taking food for a picnic and just…it'd be like people did on Earth that was, once upon a time. What the first Eden must have been like. Your colleague is a lucky girl, if that's the day you have planned for her tomorrow. Because if I got to pick a dream date, that would be it." Nihal ducked her head, then started loading dirty glasses into a dishwashing rack.

Orel sucked in a breath. He'd been completely honest with her up until now, so he couldn't bring himself to lie. "I don't have a date for tomorrow. My colleague…she…had other plans. So if I visit the rose garden tomorrow, I'll probably only fall asleep and get sunburned all over again. So by this time tomorrow, I'll be even greener."

She laughed. "You should set an alarm, so you wake up before you get burned. Or take me with you, so I can tell you funny stories to keep you from falling asleep."

His heart soared. "I'd like that. Except…well, just like with the sunbeds, you get more vitamin D the more your skin is exposed to the light, so you'd probably see a lot more of me than is usually on display."

To his surprise, Nihal grinned. "So I'd find out the answer to the question I've been dying to ask since you walked into Forge tonight – whether you're green all the way down? You never know. The sight might get me so excited, I'll lie down on the rug with you and risk a bit of exposure of my own. If only to find out more about those special skills you mentioned."

Orel's heart sank. She just wanted him for his venom, like everyone else. Once she'd had a taste of it, she'd see they weren't compatible and if he was lucky, he'd never see her again. If he wasn't lucky, he would see her again, happily partnered with someone else who wasn't affected by Cupid's curse.

But if he got to share a day with her in the Alvarium, just seeing the joy on her face at all the flowers would be worth it. He'd already offered her a shot of venom – if she took it from him in the throes of passion, what was wrong with that? Well, if she wanted that, of course. Maybe all she wanted was a picnic.

As if sensing his doubts, Nihal added, "Seeing as you're providing the ambience and the flowers, I'll see about bringing the picnic. Siofra will probably make the food, not me, but I'll see if I can rustle up something special for us to drink. Anything but fake rose fizz."

The sensible part of Orel's brain told him he should refuse. But the words that came out of his mouth were, "Sure. So I'll pick you up at eleven tomorrow? Where? Here?"

Nihal nodded. "Here's probably best. I have

to be here to accept a couple of deliveries tomorrow morning, but I should be finished by eleven."

Orel swallowed. "It's a date, then." Reluctantly, he turned to go.

"Wait, you forgot your flower!" Nihal held out the stasis rose. Cupping it in both hands like a precious treasure.

He stared at the flower for a long moment, then lifted his gaze to her face. She already valued it more than he ever could.

"It's yours," he said finally. "And tomorrow, you'll have a fresh memory of the scent to go with it."

NINETEEN

Orel spread a picnic blanket out in the rose garden, before taking a quick inventory of what food was already available in the Alvarium. Most of the bioengineers gave the place a wide berth, too afraid of the bees, so they had no idea if the watermelons were ripe until he plopped one on the break room table.

Today, he intended to offer the fresh fruit to Nihal first, seeing as she didn't see it as often as the Eden residents. Something he should be working harder to fix, in his opinion. The more food crops that went into full agricultural production to feed the people of the Colony, the better. They couldn't live off ration bars forever – there was only a finite supply of the things.

There were a couple of watermelons ready for harvest, and plenty of strawberries ripe enough to eat. The passionfruit vines weren't fruiting yet, and the stonefruit trees were still too young to do much more than grow leaves and flowers.

It was a pity the hives had been emptied only a few weeks ago, or he'd have asked the apiarist to do it today, so Nihal could have some fresh honey, too.

His comm chimed. Speak of the devil…it was Helvia the apiarist. "Hiya," he said as Helvia's face filled the screen.

"Orel, are you busy? Because I need your help. The tropical hives have all tripled production in the last month with the new bees, so I'm only half done processing the harvest, but the store room's already full from the last harvest. A couple of our regular clients are on the waitlist for increased quota when it's available, and one of them's already expecting an order today, so if you could get these three pallets over to Forge this morning, another three to the Moon and Sixpence this afternoon, and the rest to the abattoir by the end of the day, I'll have room to breathe again."

"What do the abattoir want with honey?" Orel asked.

Helvia shrugged. "Something about combining it with spices and mixing it with some of the processed, vat grown meats and plant proteins to make it easier to cook and give it more flavour. Chicken nuggets, beef burgers, veggie patties, that sort of thing. Stuff people can just put in the oven or the grill, and it comes out ready to eat. Apparently it extends the life of the meat, too — as a natural preservative."

"Oh. That actually makes sense." He

thought of the little beef morsels he'd devoured last night, smothered in a delicious sweet sauce. He was willing to bet that's what Forge's chef used the honey for. "Right, I'll take the Forge order over myself this morning, and book a couple of general labourers to transport the rest after lunch. Anything else you need from me while you've got me? I'm taking the afternoon off, so anything else will have to wait until tomorrow."

Helvia paused to think for a moment, before shaking her head. "No, I think I'm good for the moment. The new, bigger hives are holding up to the increased capacity, and the processor's getting through the raw honey as fast as I can get the buckets in place. Thanks for sourcing those. Oh, wait…do we have a destination for the leftover beeswax, or should I put it into the recycler?"

Beeswax…that definitely rang a bell. Now where had he seen it mentioned lately? Beeswax and botanical oils…

"I think we had a requisition form cross my

desk asking for beeswax, among other things. I think it was for beauty treatments or something. Leave it with me and I'll get back to you by the end of the week. In the meantime, better keep it."

"I don't have anywhere to put it!"

"I'll be right up to take those three pallets, which will leave you more than enough space, I'm sure," Orel said. At least Helvia was more reasonable than Rocail in her demands. Maybe he could ask her for a reference…

"All right. See you soon, then." Helvia ended the call.

Orel fired off his labour request before putting his tablet back in his pocket.

Now he had an important choice to make. Should he dress for his date now, or stay in his green coverall until he'd made the delivery, and then get changed? Decisions, decisions…

TWENTY

One more delivery, and Nihal could go get dressed up. She couldn't remember the last time she'd been this excited about a date. The honey delivery was due at ten, which should give her almost an hour to shower and change and do her hair and makeup. If it was late, she'd give the delivery guy a piece of her mind.

At five minutes to ten, the loading dock bell chimed.

"Your timing is so good, I could kiss you!"

she said as she palmed open the loading dock door.

Only to find herself face to face with…Orel.

He looked as nervous as she felt, but he still wore a smile. "Sorry I'm early, but when I saw the honey order for Forge due to go out this morning, I figured you'd like it sooner rather than later."

"That's where I've seen you before!" Nihal exclaimed. "I just didn't recognise you because you're not normally green. Or you are, but…your clothes, not what's underneath. You're the honey boy!"

He looked affronted. "I'm no one's honey boy. I earn a decent living in Eden, thank you very much, and…"

She shook her head. "No, you're the guy who delivers the honey here from Eden. I've seen you once or twice when I come in early on my days off."

He appeared to relax. "Oh. Yeah, that's me. Eden's errand boy, doing whatever the more important bioengineers are too busy to do."

His brow wrinkled. "What does a bar use so much honey for?"

Her lecturers at university had drilled into her how important it was to keep her brew techniques and recipes private, never to share them with anyone but her apprentices, if she chose to. But right now, she wanted to ignore the whole paranoid lot of them and invite Orel into the cellar.

"Help me take these down to the cellar, and I'll show you. Maybe even give you a taste," she said. And a kiss, her traitorous mind added with devilish glee.

"Sure."

TWENTY-ONE

Orel floated the pallets into the service elevator, then waited for Nihal to press the button for Basement Level Two.

"What's on Level One?" he asked.

"The fizz factory, where I cook up the flavour syrups in the lab before hooking them up to the mixing stations to carbonate them and bring them down to a drinkable dilution before bottling. That's where Vulcan keeps the old Earth wine stock, too, in a climate controlled vault. It's pretty full now the new stock has come in – salvaged from a vessel that went missing during the war. Trust me, you don't need to see that." She gave a delicate shudder. "I lost a bottle when I was bottling a couple days ago. It just slipped out of my hands and rolled away under the vats. Now the whole place stinks of syrup and vinegar and I haven't had time to find the bottle, or send someone in to clean up the mess. It almost makes we wish we still used robots. I could send a sweeping and mopping unit in there and have it cleaned in an hour."

"What about Level Three?"

She shrugged. "That's still empty, though if the boss has his way, like he usually does, it'll be the home of our new winemaking business in the short term, before it expands big enough to need larger premises. I'll be the winemaker, brewing and experimenting and doing what I usually do. Vulcan will provide the capital and the premises, his not inconsiderable business acumen, as well as Forge for our market research.

"He's promised me a third partner, too, who can handle the logistics and help with the business and production side of things. I mean, I can perfect the recipes for small batches I can prepare by hand, but when we're talking full-scale production, providing enough wine for the entire Colony plus surplus to export to the rest of the system, that's more than I'm willing to handle. I have my limits.

"Vulcan could probably handle it, if he wanted to – he's a master at managing a million moving parts. You should see him on stage – breathtaking. But he has his hands full with Forge and it's only a matter of time before he gives in and goes back to his real passion. He was in the Alba Academy of Dance before the rebellion, and I know he'd love to be one of the founding members of the Altan Academy, when he gets around to organising it. If anyone can convince the Senate to fund an institution like that, it's him, but I think he wants the wine business to give him the financial freedom to finance it on his own. That's why we need a third partner, someone to run the business when Vulcan steps back. He'll find someone perfect, I know it – it's what he does."

He sounded like the opposite of Rocail. "I wish my boss was half as good as yours. I'd struggle to say anything good about him, except that he's an expert in his field. But so's everyone in Eden. Well, except me. That's why I'm everyone's errand boy, dealing with all the details no one else knows how to handle. Order the new equipment. Organise this delivery. Set up a supply chain. Take this experimental plant or beastie and teach a farmer to put it into production. Not that the last one happens often. Did you know only a tenth of the Colony's farm facilities are being used? If we put it all into production tomorrow, the whole Colony would be eating fresh food every day by the end of the year."

She stared at him. "Why don't we, then?"

Orel shrugged. "Beats me. Politics, or secret

agendas, or something else I just don't understand. Or maybe it's meant to be my job, but my time's so eaten up with deliveries, random requests, and sourcing strange, new lab equipment every other day, that I never have a moment to actually do it." He found he'd clenched his fists so hard his nails were digging into his palms. Orel forced himself to relax, blowing out a breath to help release the tension. "I'm sorry. I didn't come here to complain about my job. I'd rather hear about yours, and then take you out for a picnic, if you're still up for it. I promise I won't whine any more today."

To his surprise, she only smiled. "Oh, but I was hoping you'd help me drink some. My job is to create the Colony's first vintages, and I'd like to hear your opinion on them. Not to mention if you wine and dine me well enough in this garden you've promised, I have plans, if you're up for them."

Yes. A thousand times yes. Even if they only had one day together before she rejected him…it would be one perfect day. Orel closed his eyes and took a deep breath. He recognised the signs – his rapid heartbeat, dry mouth…stars, he could almost feel his pupils dilating, so he could drink her in with more clarity, to remember…

Signs he'd seen in so many others as they fell deeply in love. He barely knew Nihal, and yet…he knew. Which would only make it harder when she didn't return his feelings. All the more reason to hold off sleeping with her, if he could. Because once she tasted his venom, he'd lose her forever. Cupid's curse sucked worse than a black hole.

The elevator doors whizzed open.

"Welcome to my lair," Nihal said, pointing. "Put the pallets over there. I'll deal with them tomorrow. I have something special in mind when my dragon fruit arrives. A sort of cider or melomel. Maybe both. I'm not sure…"

She proceeded to point out tanks that she said held beer, rice wine and mead, before picking up a bottle off the shelf. "This is what

I did with your honey." She shook the bottle a little, and froth formed in the neck. "It's a sparkling mead. I used champagne yeast, and the result is surprisingly similar to the Earth wines Vulcan keeps in the vault. I have a couple of bottles of this chilling upstairs for us, if you'd like to try it. Some beer, too, in case you'd prefer that."

How could he tell her he didn't care what the picnic included, as long as she was there?

"I'm ready to go when you are," he said.

TWENTY-TWO

Orel palmed the door open, then stood to the side to let Nihal enter the biome first.

"What's an...Alvarium?" she asked, squinting up at the sign.

"It means beehive in Latin, but it also means womb. I think it's named after the first one, though," Orel said.

"So this is where my honey comes from?"

"Some of it, yes. Today's delivery came from one of the tropical biomes. I don't know which one."

Why was she hesitating? Didn't she want to go inside? Did she want to leave?

Nihal turned to face him, a sheepish smile on her face. "Can you believe I'm nervous? You don't know how long I've dreamed about seeing a real garden again." She closed her eyes, took a deep breath, then spun on the spot and stepped inside.

"Oh, Orel, it's beautiful. I've never seen anything like it outside pictures from Earth. Tito didn't have anything like this." She turned a slow circle, taking it all in. Joy lit her face, brighter than the sunlamps above.

He wanted to take her in his arms and kiss her. He wanted to take out his tablet and take a picture, so he'd remember this moment. He wanted…

She threw her arms around his neck and kissed him. As soon as it started, it was over, but in that one precious moment, he knew she was nothing like Fancy the succubus.

Nihal let out a breathless laugh. "Sorry.

That's for bringing me here. I could stand here all day, just looking, and it would rank right up there as my best date ever."

He moistened his mouth. "You haven't even seen the rose garden yet."

She reached for his hand, her fingers warm as they wove between his. "Show me."

Luckily his feet knew the way, because his brain was focussed wholly on her. The way her smile lit her whole face, the warmth of her hand in his, the brush of her leg against his, a heated touch even through both of their clothes...

"So this is where it happened. On this very rug?" She sat down, patting the spot beside her.

Orel set down the catering box that held their promised picnic and stretched out on the rug. "I was lying here like this," he said.

Nihal laughed. "Oh, that can't be right. You said something about being exposed. Surely you were wearing less clothing. Show me."

"I was naked, Nihal. Are you sure you want

that? Before we've had lunch?" Please say no. Please let him have just a little bit longer before she left.

She held up her hand, her finger and thumb almost touching. "I was this close to offering to share one of the double capsules with you last night. You never did tell me about your special skills."

So she didn't know. Orel blew out a breath. "It's not skills so much as…when I get aroused, I have less control over my venom secretion. So it ends up all over my hands and what with all the kissing and touching, in the heat of the moment…you're bound to end up with some in your mouth. It only takes a drop. You'll feel your perception sharpening, seeing so much more than you did before, and that's when Cupid's curse kicks in, because cupids are immune to the venom. You won't want me any more – I'll be nothing to you. You'll want the partner who's your perfect match, and you won't settle for less. I know I offered you a taste last night, and I will keep my word, but...I want to be selfish just a little bit longer, and enjoy your company while I can. Even if it's just as long as lunch lasts."

Nihal tipped onto her back and actually rolled around laughing on the rug. "Seriously? You don't want to sleep with me because you like me? What if I told you that I didn't pour that glass down the sink last night, and instead, I drank it all? I've had eyes for no one else but you since you walked into my bar last night — not even Prometheus. I wanted to know if you were green all over, especially after I heard the whole story. I wanted to drag Fancy off you and kick her out of the bar. And I want to get naked with you right now, venom or no venom, because no matter how much I want to smell the roses, I want you more. So stars take your imaginary Cupid's curse, because I am breaking it, right here, right now." Her eyes burned. "Tell me if I'm wrong. Tell me I imagined the attraction between us last night, and today. Tell me you don't want me as much as I want you. Tell me all those things, and I'll

go open that picnic basket and have lunch."
She made it sound like lunch was something
that belonged in the sewers.

His voice seemed to have died, and what
was left came out in a whisper. "I can't. I can't
believe it, but I can't."

TWENTY-THREE

Nihal's heart sank as she squeezed her eyes shut. She'd messed up. Should have said stuff differently, not reminded him of Fancy last night, maybe even had lunch like a normal date, not some lovesick fool…

Something landed softly on the blanket beside her. Her eyes flew open, to see Orel's shirt. His pants followed it, before he stuck his hands into the waistband of his shorts.

"I was naked, lying right here on this rug."

Off came the shorts. Yep, green all the way down. "Lying here on my side, like this." He faced away from her, his peachy green arse on full display. "And with the solar lamps all over the dome above, angled to give the most light to all the plants below, I burned pretty much all of me except the side I was lying on. Of course, when I grabbed the healing salve, I slathered it on everywhere I could reach, not caring if it was a burned bit or not. Until the next day, when I realised it wouldn't wash off…" He twisted his head so she could see his face. "This might just be the craziest thing I've ever done."

Nihal wet her lips. "Love apparently makes people crazy." She sat up, so she could pull off her shirt. Then her pants, followed by her underwear, piled up next to his. Before she could lose her nerve, she straddled him, and he rolled onto his back to meet her halfway. His hard, green length lay between her thighs, but her focus was on his face, as he stared at her in wonder. Before she could second guess herself, she seized his hand and sucked on his fingers, one at a time, slow and languorous, before doing the same with the other hand.

Still holding his gaze, the ground her hips against him. Back and forth, with torturous slowness, feeling the heat building, far too fast, until it seemed something inside her exploded in the best way.

It took several long moments before she could both breathe and see again, or ask, "What in the stars was that?"

"I think…it's something I've heard about but never seen…may I?" His hand hovered over her breast. She nodded wordlessly. He cupped her breast gently, even that slight touch leaving her gasping, before his tongue touched her nipple. Then his mouth closed over it and she screamed until she ran out of breath.

He waited for her to recover before he continued, "I think…you know how I said the venom makes you more perceptive? Especially around your…love interest. It heightens your perceptions, your senses, so if you find them, while the venom is still in your system, and get intimate…it heightens that, too. I thought it was a myth, but…I barely touched you, and…" His hand hovered over her breast again, as if not daring to touch her again, in case she screamed.

Stars take that. "Do it again." When he hesitated, she added, "The other nipple this time."

More sure of her now, he sucked hard, without warning. She felt the orgasm build before time stopped.

"This shouldn't be possible," Orel breathed.

Stars, even his breath across her sensitive skin was enough to send her into an upward spiral. Three orgasms in as many minutes. No, it shouldn't be possible, but the evidence said otherwise. If the foreplay was this good, what about the sex?

"I want to feel you inside me. Now," she said. "I'm going to fuck your curse into a black hole. We make our own myths here.

Together."

Wonder and disbelief warred in his eyes for a moment, before they somehow merged into resolve. "Together," he breathed, as he thrust inside her.

"Yes. Oh, yes. Yes. Stars, yes. Orel, oh, Orel, I'm about to…I'm going to…oh, stars, yes!"

TWENTY-FOUR

When Nihal returned to Forge, she'd hoped to have a few minutes to catch her breath before having to deal with people again. Yesterday and the night that followed with Orel had been unbelievable. She couldn't wait to see him again.

"Good afternoon. How'd the singles thing go?"

Vulcan leaned against the bar, taking her in over his folded arms.

She tried to keep her voice nonchalant. "Fairly smoothly. Some people got lucky, Fancy didn't…oh, and I think I may have found our third business partner for the wholesale wine business." Okay, a little bit of excitement had crept into her tone there, but that was to be expected.

"Oh? Does he have anything to do with why you're looking distinctly green today?"

Stars. Of course Vulcan had noticed.

"Oh, that. I fell asleep in a sunbed yesterday. The green's from the healing balm I had to use on the sunburn." She tried not to think of Orel's hands smoothing the balm over her skin. She'd never known first aid could be so erotic.

"Or why you're walking stiffly?"

A dozen orgasms in a night would do that to a girl. Not to mention the ones during the day…

"Sunburn, like I told you."

"Uh-huh. So, when do I get to meet this partner of yours? Do I know him?" Stars, but

Vulcan sounded like her father might have, if he'd been here.

"He works in Eden, and he's a perfect match. Ideal, really. He's quite interested in the project, though I haven't officially asked him if he wants to be part of it. We were busy with…other things." She hoped the green tint on her skin hid her blush.

From Vulcan's expression, she guessed it didn't. "I bet. You know, it's usually not a good idea to sleep with your business partner. Unless he's more than just a business partner."

"Oh, yes." The words slipped out before she could think.

Vulcan grinned. "See? I told you singles events aren't all bad. Sometimes you get lucky."

And sometimes Cupid's arrow lands exactly where it's supposed to.

Best Valentine's Day ever. Until next year…

ABOUT THE AUTHOR

Demelza Carlton has always loved the ocean, but on her first snorkelling trip she found she was afraid of fish.

She has since swum with sea lions, sharks and sea cucumbers and stood on spray drenched cliffs over a seething sea as a seven-metre cyclonic swell surged in, shattering a shipwreck below.

Demelza now lives in Perth, Western Australia, the shark attack capital of the world.

The *Ocean's Gift* series was her first foray into fiction, followed by her suspense thriller *Nightmares* trilogy. She swears the *Mel Goes to Hell* series ambushed her on a crowded train and wouldn't leave her alone.

Want to know more? You can follow Demelza on Facebook, Twitter, YouTube or her website, Demelza Carlton's Place at:

<u>www.demelzacarlton.com</u>

More Books by Demelza Carlton

<u>Colony: Holiday series</u>

Cowboys and Aliens (#1)

Ghost (#2)

Vulcan (#3)

Cupid (#4)

Valentine(#5)

Prometheus (#6)

<u>**Colony: Aqua series**</u>

Halcyon (#1)

Poseidon (#2)

Apollo (#3)

<u>**Nightmares Trilogy**</u>

Nightmares of Caitlin Lockyer (#1)

Necessary Evil of Nathan Miller (#2)

Afterlife of Alana Miller (#3)

<u>**Mel Goes to Hell series**</u>

The Devil's Work (#1)

See You in Hell (#2)

Mel Goes to Hell (#3)

To Hell and Back (#4)

The Holiday From Hell (#5)

All Hell Breaks Loose (#6)

The Devil Goes to Heaven (#7)

<u>**Romance Island Resort series**</u>

Maid for the Rock Star (#1)

The Rock Star's Email Order Bride (#2)

The Rock Star's Virginity (#3)

The Rock Star and the Billionaire (#4)

The Rock Star Wants A Wife (#5)

The Rock Star's Wedding (#6)

Maid for the South Pole (#7)

<u>Romance a Medieval Fairytale series</u>

Enchant: Beauty and the Beast Retold

Dance: Cinderella Retold

Fly: Goose Girl Retold

Revel: Twelve Dancing Princesses
Retold

Silence: Little Mermaid Retold

Awaken: Sleeping Beauty Retold

Embellish: Brave Little Tailor Retold

Appease: Princess and the Pea Retold

Blow: Three Little Pigs Retold

Return: Hansel and Gretel Retold

Wish: Aladdin Retold

Melt: Snow Queen Retold

Spin: Rumpelstiltskin Retold

Kiss: Frog Prince Retold

Reflect: Snow White Retold

Roar: Goldilocks Retold

Cobble: Elves and the Shoemaker Retold

Float: Enchanted Horse Retold

Steal: Forty Thieves Retold

Call: Pied Piper Retold
Fall: Scheherazade Retold
Feather: Swan Maidens Retold
Cross: Billy Goats Gruff Retold
Weave: Rapunzel Retold
Claim: Puss in Boots Retold
Curse: Rose Red Retold

* 9 7 8 1 9 2 5 7 9 9 4 3 9 *